Mindful Nature

For Calbee, who keeps me mindful—*PT*

Cover photo credits: Coleman, Adrian. (2020). *Harvest mouse* [Photograph]. iStock.

Published by Magination Press in partnership with National Wildlife Federation
maginationpress.org and nwf.org

Distributed by Lerner Publisher Services
lernerbooks.com

Written by Paige Towler
Edited by Katie ten Hagen and Julie Spalding
Book design by Chris Gaugler
Produced by WonderLab Group LLC
Printed by Corporate Graphics, North Mankato, MN

Library of Congress Cataloging-in-Publication Data

Names: Towler, Paige, author.
Title: Mindful nature: connecting with our great green world/Paige Towler.
Description: Washington DC : Magination Press, [2025] | Audience term: Children | Audience term: School children | Summary: "A beautiful, calming blend of thought prompts and stunning nature photography to create a truly absorbing and meditative experience for young readers"–Provided by publisher.
Identifiers: LCCN 2024032919 (print) | LCCN 2024032920 (ebook) | ISBN 9781433845185 (hardback) | ISBN 9781433845192 (ebook)
Subjects: LCSH: Mindfulness (Psychology)–Juvenile literature. | Emotions–Juvenile literature. | Nature–Juvenile literature.
Classification: LCC BF637.M56 T69 2025 (print) | LCC BF637.M56 (ebook) | DDC 158.1/3–dc23/eng/20240815
LC record available at https://lccn.loc.gov/2024032919
LC ebook record available at https://lccn.loc.gov/2024032920

Manufactured in the United States of America

10 9 8 7 6 5 4 3 2 1

Mindful Nature

Connecting With Our Great Green World

PAIGE TOWLER

MAGINATION PRESS • WASHINGTON, DC
AMERICAN PSYCHOLOGICAL ASSOCIATION

Rise and shine, *harvest* mouse. Your cozy blossom bed is speckled with fresh dew.

Breathe deeply.

Can you smell

the sweet scent of the flower?

Relax, *little meerkat.*
The smooth sand is
warm on your belly.

Take a big yawn.

Wiggle your toes

against the ground.

Feel the earth around you.

Swish. Stretch your arms out wide like an owl in flight.

Bring your wings up, up, up

and gently back down.

Breathe in and out.

Hoot softly as you imagine gliding through the chilled air.

The bear stretches roly-poly in the shimmering sunlight. Its fur is thick and soft.

Spread your

fingers

and toes

wide.

Reach your fingers toward your toes.

Make a strong growling noise.

Playful foxes move through the meadow. Their cool, wet noses meet. Boop!

Touch your finger to your nose.

Wiggle your ears.

Imagine you
have a long,
sleek tail.

What games
will you play?

Golden grass ripples under endless blue sky. Where are the elephants going?

Imagine you are on a journey alongside them.

Breathe in.

Breathe out.

Make the shushing sound

of dry grasses in warm winds.

The sun is hot.
The shade is cool.
Lounge like a leopard
stretched on a strong branch.

Imagine the feeling of tree bark.

Leaves

rustle

all

around.

What can you see from up high in a tree?

Hush. Cold, clean snow **drifts down.**

Trace the deer's large ears.

Shh. Can you hear the silence?

Tap, tap, tap.

Soft, warm rain patters over the frog.

Tap your fingertips against your skin.

Can you feel the raindrops?

The otters *slide* together through cool waters.

Wrap your arms around yourself
or hug someone close by.

Close your eyes.

Imagine you are

floating weightlessly.

What does it feel like to
move with the waves?

Brilliant birds swing side by side on branches.

Count the birds.

Stroke their bright feathers.

Sway gently like a bird on the branch.

A sunset sky turns yellow and pink above a *soft seal pup*.

The ice is crisp and white.

Close your eyes.

What colors do you see?

The woods are waiting.
Quiet fireflies light the way.

Walk your

fingers up

the path.

Close your eyes.

Imagine where it leads.

Reader's Note

by Julia Martin Burch, PhD

Notice the weight of this book in your hands. Study the contrast of the light type against the dark paper. Can you smell any scents? What sounds do the turning pages make? As you reflect on these questions, you are practicing mindfulness! The term mindfulness has grown in popularity in recent years and is commonly confused with mediation, stillness, or having an empty, quiet mind. Yet, being mindful simply means paying attention to the present moment, on purpose, without judging your experience as good or bad. By this definition, you can practice mindfulness during calm, quiet activities, like a meerkat enjoying a stretch on the warm sand. But you can be just as mindfully present chasing fireflies down a wooded path or wrestling like wild otter pups in the water.

Mindfulness, Nature, and Kids

Children have an incredible innate ability to become mindfully absorbed in the world around them, and the natural world presents endless opportunities to observe its intricacies! As busy adults, we often find ourselves moving quickly through the world around us, but if we can pause for a moment and fully attend to nature with our senses, as children often do instinctively, we reap a host of benefits. Though the study of mindfulness and nature is still growing, research has found that time spent in nature can improve physical health, in ways such as lowering blood pressure and improving immune functioning, refreshing fatigued attention and focus, and reducing stress, depression, and anxiety.

How to Be Mindful in Nature

Foster your child's innate curiosity for the natural world by trying to see nature through their eyes. For example, lie on your bellies side-by-side and watch an ant hill teeming with life. When you or your child notice your mind wandering or feelings like boredom arising, try naming those experiences without judgment ("ah, here's boredom!" or "My mind is busy making lists") and then choose to return your focus on the present moment. Every time you intentionally bring your attention back to the present, you build your mindfulness "muscle," making you a more aware, intentional person in the long term.

Let's Practice!

As you read this book with your child, complete the activities together. Ask them how they feel in their bodies or what emotions they notice when they try the activities. You can lead by example, such as sharing "I notice that my muscles relax, my breath is slower, and I feel happy and calm when we read this book. What do you notice?" This self-reflection helps your child build awareness of their own feelings, thoughts, and physical sensations—a key component of mindfulness.

Get out into nature with your child! You can help your child build their mindfulness muscle by simply getting them out and engaged in the natural world. Help them notice what it feels like to fully attend to the world around them, using all of their senses. This can be as simple as detouring through your local park on the way to school or a bigger excursion like a trip to your local pond, beach, field, or forest. When you're out in nature, try some of the following:

- Go for a mindful nature walk. Choose one sense to focus on. Walk through nature while fully focusing on that sense. For example, if you chose vision, what do you notice about the colors and shapes of the plants around you? What is the light like? How long are the shadows? How do trees move when the wind blows? Mindfully engaging with our senses is a portable and potent way to ground ourselves in nature.
- Find a "sit spot." Allow your child to choose their very own special spot outdoors to sit and observe. Return to the spot regularly to notice how nature changes slowly, but steadily. Some children enjoy simply studying the resident insects in their sit spot, while others like a bit more engagement, such as drawing the spot as it changes with the seasons or doing a nature craft like braiding grass or making daisy chains.
- Collect leaves, flowers, ferns, and other natural items to press in a book or to make crayon or charcoal rubbings from. Get curious with your child about the details of the plant that they notice on the paper compared to the original item.
- Go on a leaf or cloud hunt and try to find leaves or clouds with interesting shapes or structures.

As you walk outside with your child, ask each other questions to deepen your engagement with the natural world around you. For example, "if this tree could speak, what might it say?" or "how long do you think that rock has been there? How many kids do you think have walked past it?" These can also be great moments to practice mindful gratitude, such as reflecting on what you appreciate most about your local natural area or hugging a tree and noticing the feel and smell of its bark.

Slowing down and mindfully enjoying nature with a child can be one of life's sweetest experiences. In the daily hustle and bustle, it's easy to miss the details around us, but the natural world provides so many opportunities. These moments can be loud and grand like the crash of waves on rocks or as quiet as the *tap tap tap* of rain on a frog's back. No matter what the moment brings, you give yourself and your child a lasting gift by intentionally tuning in and mindfully attending to the natural world.

Paige Towler lives in Washington, DC. Her poetry and writings have appeared in many anthologies, and she has written books for National Geographic, Britannica Books, Scholastic, Union Square & Co, and more.

Julia Martin Burch, PhD is a clinical child psychologist and the founder and director of Do What Works, a group practice dedicated to providing evidence-based treatment to young people and their parents. Dr. Martin Burch is also passionate about sharing effective parenting techniques through workshops, consulting, and writing.

Books for Kids from APA

The American Psychological Association works to advance psychology as a science and profession, as a means to improve health and human welfare. APA publishes books for young readers under its imprint, Magination Press. It's the combined power of psychology and literature that helps kids navigate life's challenges more easily. Visit maginationpress.org and @MaginationPress on Facebook, X, Instagram, and Pinterest.

The National Wildlife Federation, America's largest and most trusted conservation organization, works across the country to unite Americans from all walks of life in giving wildlife a voice. NWF has been on the front lines for wildlife since 1936, fighting for the conservation values that are woven into the fabric of our nation's collective heritage. NWF is also a publisher of magazines for children. For over 55 years, Ranger Rick has aimed to inspire in its readers a greater understanding of the natural world, a deep love of nature and wildlife, and a lasting commitment to conservation and environmental action.

Photo Credits

p1: rob_lan. (2013). *Rainy day* [Photograph]. iStock.
p4-5: Coleman, Adrian. (2020). *Harvest mouse* [Photograph]. iStock.
p6-7: Nichetti, Luca (2017). *Meerkat stretching and yawning on red sand* [Photograph]. Shutterstock.
p8-9: Mandel, Missy (2015) National Wildlife Federation.
p10-11: Bentlage, Hank (2009). *Cute little brown bear waving with its paw at you* [Photograph]. iStock.
p12-13: Freeborn, Kathleen (2007) National Wildlife Federation.
p14-15: Anagramm (2014). *African elephant with calf stock photo* [Photograph]. iStock.
p16-17: Martin Mecnarowski, Martin (n.d.). *Sri Lankan leopard* [Photograph]. Shutterstock.
p18-19: Rudd, Connie (2017) National Wildlife Federation.
p20-21: BBA Photography (n.d.). *White's Tree Frog (Litoria caerulea) in the rain* [Photograph]. Shutterstock.
p22-23: Green, Danny (2020). *Sea otter (Enhydra lutris) female and pup playing* [Photograph]. Nature Picture Library.
p24-25: Blackwell, Peter. (2006). *Seven Little Bee-eaters (Merops pusillus) in a row, one facing away, Masai Mara, Kenya* [Photograph]. Nature Picture Library.
p26-27: Rollins, John (2014) National Wildlife Federation.
p28-29: tdub303 (2016). *Fireflies light up the forest at night* [Photograph]. iStock.
p30-31: Laskarakis, Panagiotis (2015) National Wildlife Federation.
Back cover: Rudd, Connie (2017) National Wildlife Federation.